Unholy Crusade

by Zoë Robinson

Unholy Crusade

First Published 2012

Copyright © 2010 Zoë Robinson
Cover design copyright © 2011 Zoë Robinson

Cataloguing and Publication Data is available from the
British Library.

ISBN 9780-9542-4558-0

Typset in Liberation Sans by All Mouse Media Ltd, Bolton
Printed and bound by Lulu.com

Published by All Mouse Media Ltd,
105 Eldon Street, Bolton BL2 2JE

www.allmousemedia.com
www.zoerobinson.com

For Jennifer,

who stood by me through thick and thin.

Also by Zoe Robinson

The Curse of the Other World

Ink Proof Cannon (comic)

With Jennifer Kirk

The Life of Nob T. Mouse (comic)

All Over the House (comic)

Unholy Crusade

Chapter One

1

A significant problem with filming the undead was that they
moved so fast it was almost impossible to be sure they were
there at all. This problem was compounded by the fact that
grainy CCTV footage was terrible at filming everyday events
even in good light. So a vampire fighting in the dark was
never going to provide Oscar-winning footage.

Nevertheless, Seth Baron sat with a mug of hot coffee in
one hand and a DVD remote in the other, watching the same
piece of film over and over again.

The footage showed a woman entering the yard of
Pearson's Holdings, a warehouse on Fenton Industrial
Estate just outside of town, during a drug deal. The
participants had taken umbrage with her arrival and
attacked. She killed three of the four men involved in the
deal, and left with the fourth man slumped over her shoulder,
unconscious.

'Who is she?' asked Tom Carter. He was a young man by
Seth's reckoning. Mid thirties, slightly receding hairline and
two kids by a wife he hardly ever saw any more.

This was just about the sum total of what Seth knew about
his partner. They had been teamed up on the last staff
rotation eight months ago but neither man liked to share
much personal information, so everything Seth knew was
gleaned from details that slipped into conversation here and
there.

'I don't know,' said Seth.

'But she's important.' It was a definite statement, not a question. Tom Carter never asked a question if he thought he already knew the answer.

Seth grunted his acknowledgement. 'Print out a copy of this frame, would you? I want to run an E-FIT, see if we can find her in the database.'

The printer in the corner of the room churned and spat out a sheet of cheap A4 with the frame of video on it. Carter handed the paper to Seth, who slipped it into a file.

Seth grabbed the remote again and let the video proceed until he found another frame he wanted. This one showed the face of the man who had survived the deal going sour. Whether he was still alive now the woman had him was another matter.

'Print that too,' said Seth. 'Let's see who our missing gentleman is.'

It took all of two hours for a basic E-FIT to be worked up for the man and the results of a cursory search through the Police National Computer to come back. He was Mark First, also known by three other names: Thomas First, Mark Jameson, and Anthony Fields. Given the repetition between the first three names, Seth was willing to go out on a limb and believe Mark First was the man's real name.

Seth sat in his office, sipping a mug of coffee, his fifth that day, and read over the report that accompanied First's summary sheet. It was not pleasant reading. First had been active in both the international assassin and the paranormal communities for well over a decade. At 45 years old, he showed no signs of slowing down. In fact if last night's escapade was anything to go by, he appeared to be diversifying even further.

There was a knock on the door. Three quick raps. Carter entered without waiting for a response.

'I got your message,' said Carter. 'Results came back positive?'

Seth tossed First's file onto the desk in front of him. 'Take a look at that.'

Carter picked up the file and flicked through its contents. It was full of photographs, police reports and newspaper clippings. 'Nice chap. Gets about a bit. He-llo! What do we have here?'

'You got to the bit about the zombies in Belize?'

Thomas nodded. He looked a little green around the gills. 'He's a pervert who's dealing now? Doesn't seem like his kind of business.'

Seth shook his head. 'Agreed. He's an assassin, not a dealer.'

'So why would he be at a drug deal?'

'For a hit?' Carter suggested. He placed the file on the desk and pointed to a cut-out from The Times. 'It wouldn't be the first time. Says here he posed as muscle for a Canadian dealer over in Quebec, then killed him after the deal went down and fled with the cash.'

'That was twenty years ago,' said Seth. 'He doesn't take risks like that any more.'

'I'm just saying it's a possibility.'

'It's more likely he was there for something they were

9

bringing in with the drugs,' said Thomas.

Seth nodded. 'Or because he knew someone would be there.'

'The girl, you mean?'

'Exactly.'

'Any news on her yet?' asked Carter.

Seth looked over at the door, saw it was closed, and pulled a sheet of paper from the top drawer in his desk. 'Sign this. It ups your security clearance.'

Carter pulled a pen from his jacket and scrawled his signature on the dotted line. 'Does it also bump up my pay grade?'

'You wish.'

Seth hunted around in his jacket for a keyring. He unlocked the top drawer in his desk and removed a red, loose-leaf file. Stamped on the cover were the words 'Top secret. KC3. Eyes only.'

He looked the other man in the eye. 'What I'm about to tell you does not leave this room. Understand?'

The younger man nodded.

Seth opened the file and took out the grainy, monochrome photograph from the top of the pile of papers inside. He handed the photograph to Carter.

'Her name is Gretl Lune,' said Seth. 'Or at least we think it is. She goes by several pseudonyms and, like First, she's a dab hand at disguises.'

Carter looked at the photograph, slipped it back into the file. 'Looks a lot like the woman from the video. So who is she?'

'Nobody knows,' said Seth as he sifted through the ream of

papers in the file. 'But here's where things get interesting.'

He selected a report and handed it over.

'This is a coroner's report for...' Carter's voice trailed off for a moment before he regained his composure. 'You've got to be joking.'

'No joke,' said Seth. 'Officially at least, Gretl Lune died in 1963.'

2

The rain bleached down, chilling the air and destroying any evidence that was still to be found on the pockmarked concrete floor. Seth stood in the middle of the warehouse yard, his umbrella providing only minimal cover from the downpour, and surveyed the scene.

Carter wondered if the old man saw something here that he could not. As far as he was concerned, the coroner's report and the site reports from the investigating officers were more than enough to go on with. No need for him to freeze his arse off in the rain too.

'Let me get this straight,' said Carter. 'We're here looking for evidence that a dead person wandered in here and killed a man police from around the world have been hunting for years?'

'That's pretty much it,' said Seth. He tried to light a cigarette but the wind was too strong for the flame to lick the tip.

Carter shone a torch around the floor, not sure what he was supposed to be looking for. Did the dead leave a trail? Would there be evidence of half-chewed brains laid around.

He was here to hunt occultists and other fraudsters, not walking corpses.

'But that makes no sense,' Carter protested. 'The dead don't go around killing people. I'd have noticed.'

'Oh I don't know about – hold on! What's that?'

Carter shone his torch at the wheel of a truck. 'I don't see anything.'

'Seth crouched by the wheel and felt under the cab. 'Got it.'

He pulled his hand back, opened his fist and shone the torch onto the palm of his hand.

Laid on the worn leather of his glove was a bullet, silver and flattened on one end. The specks of dried blood covering its surface began to liquify in the rain and run off onto his palm.

3

Back in the relative warmth of the car, Seth turned the packet over in his hand and stared at it. Silver alloy. Compacted tip.

'Hollowpoint?' he asked.

Carter shook his head. 'Unlikely. It hasn't fractured.'

'Something doesn't add up here,' said Seth. 'If it's solid, there's no payload. If there's no payload, he couldn't kill her. We're missing something.'

'This is definitely from his gun?' asked Carter.

'Think of the ballistics. It was fired in the wrong direction for her to have used it.'

Seth clenched his fist around the bullet in its packet. The

younger man looked at him expectantly. 'Maybe the police found something?'

'Maybe. Get their report.'

Seth stuffed the packet into the inside pocket of his jacket and pulled on his seatbelt.

'And put out a search for anyone matching Lune's description,' said Seth. 'Maybe we'll get lucky and find where she's been hiding.'

4

The police report revealed nothing of use. Seth dropped it onto his desk, ran a hand through his hair and sighed deeply.

'So close,' he said, talking to himself.

He looked over at the window, saw his reflection; the night sky turning the glass into a mirror. His gaunt face, all thin wire glasses and grey-black stubble, stared back at him through tired eyes. God, he looked old. When had that happened?

He reached into the lower drawer in his desk and pulled out a bottle of *Glenlivet*. The bottle had been a birthday present from his son. It still had a message attached, tied around the neck with a piece of string.

Happy fiftieth, Dad. Here's something to finish off your liver with.

He had intended to open it when he caught the bastard who killed his son, but that would not happen now. He was in the police morgue. That bitch Lune had got to him first.

He looked at the bottle. It glinted in the light from his desk lamp. No sense leaving it to collect dust in a drawer any longer. Time to toast the memory of dead children.

At least someone had brought Craig's killer down. It should have been him, but at least it wasn't old age.

He was about to open the bottle when someone knocked on his door. The bottle clinked enticingly as he slipped it back into the drawer.

'Come in,' he said.

Carter entered, holding a pale blue file.

'You're still here?' asked Seth. 'I thought everyone had gone home.'

'This just came in,' said Carter. He was smiling as he handed over the file.

Seth flicked through it, scanning the pages quickly; absorbing the gist. He looked up and smiled.

'I've already called Thomas,' said Carter. 'He'll meet us there.'

Chapter Two

1

Jeremy Pellier poured himself a double whisky, downed it in one, and poured himself another. His hands were shaking. The bottle clinked against the glass.

He needed to pull himself together and the alcohol was not helping. It should. It always used to. It was not.

How could this have happened? he asked himself.

Lights glided across the bar. Outside, gravel crunched beneath heavy wheels. An engine ticked over, then turned off.

He downed the whisky, pushed himself away from the counter and headed over to one of the plush leather chairs beside the fire. It was better if they found him looking relaxed than cowering over a bottle.

Low voices murmured at the door. He could not hear what they were saying. The front door closed. A moment later there was a knock on the study door.

'Enter!' he called. He hoped his voice was steady.

Dupont entered, flanked by two men in grey suits. Jeremy stood up, smiled a warm smile.

'Monsieur Dupont,' said Jeremy. 'How nice to see you again.'

'I wish I could say the same,' said Dupont. His thick Parisian accent made his words difficult to understand. 'I assume you know why I am here.'

Dupont walked over to one of the leather chairs and sat down.

Lost for words, Jeremy sat down also.

'Now,' said Dupont, fixing Jeremy with a stare that bore through him. 'Explain to me exactly what happened tonight.'

Jeremy sat forward, resting his elbows on his thighs. 'Why don't you tell me.'

'Tell you what?'

'Oh, I don't know. How about *why you sold us out?*'

Dupont's associates shifted marginally closer to their boss. Dupont raised a black-gloved hand. The men backed off again.

'I did no such thing,' said Dupont.

'They knew we were coming!' Jeremy shouted. 'I was lucky to get out of there with my skin.'

'This was not my doing.'

'Then who's was it? Nobody else knew about this meeting.'

'Monsieur Pellier, my associates and I are not in the business of selling out those we are trying to do business with. It does not make... how do you say it? "Good financial sense". If there was a problem with security, it came from your side, not ours.'

'All my men were totally trustworthy.'

'Were you followed?'

'Of course not! I'm not a fucking amateur.'

'Then I suggest either you pay closer attention to those you associate with, or you get better security. It is clear to me that you either have a mole, or a spy.' Dupont stood up. 'Either way, our business here is concluded. Good evening, Monsieur Pellier.'

As the men walked to the door Jeremy leapt to his feet. 'Now just a fucking minute!'

Dupont turned around slowly. 'There is nothing more to discuss.'

'I'm out two million on this fucking deal. I lost good men tonight, loyal men, and more product than I care to think about right now.'

'That is your concern, Monsieur, not mine.'

Dupont walked out, his guards blocking the door so Jeremy could not follow.

'This isn't over!' Jeremy shouted. 'You fucking hear me, you French bastard!'

He stood at the window and watched Dupont's car drive away, then pulled the telephone from his pocket and called Reggie Dixon.

'Pellie, my son,' said Reggie. 'Tell me you've got good news.'

'Sorry, boss. The frog didn't want to hear any of it. Said it was our fault the deal went south, then left.'

'He's an arrogant prick but he'll learn some manners pretty sharpish when I'm through with him.'

'What do you want me to do, boss? He said we've got a Wally.'

'You do nothing, sunshine. That little prick thinks he's a big boy now he's in with the kraut. Just get back here *tout sweet.*'

Reggie hung up. Jeremy slipped the telephone back into his jacket and poured himself another drink.

Chapter Three

1

Carter drove at just under the speed limit, saying little. The radio played the kind of jazz music that only people into music nobody else liked would ever want to hear; as it often did at this time of night.

Seth sat in silence, half listening to the awful music, half staring blankly ahead and trying not to get his hopes up. This could well be a dead end.

The rain was easing off when the car pulled up behind a blue Ford. Seth recognised the registration number. Thomas had already arrived.

Carter nodded toward a building a few metres further down the road. 'That's the place. Third floor.'

Seth looked over at the building. It looked like just another crumbling high rise, the kind that had looked like a beacon of progress and modern living for three weeks in the 1960s and now looked like the scum-filled sewer pit it was. It, like the rest of the neighbourhood, needed tearing down and building properly. Not that this would ever happen, he told himself. Too much profit in building on the cheap, then demolishing and rebuilding on the cheap later.

A window on the second floor shone light out into the street through thin curtains. The rest of the building was lifeless: no lights, no open windows, no sign of activity at all.

Carter pulled a gun from his shoulder holster and checked it.

'You won't need that,' said Seth.

'It makes me feel better.'

'Just don't go for it. It won't do you any good.'

'Yeah. I got that much from the CCTV.'

The younger man slipped the gun back into its holster and they both climbed out of the car.

Carter pulled his coat tighter around himself and turned up his collar. 'Bloody rain. Feels like it's been raining for days.'

Seth walked over to the blue Ford and knocked on the driver's side window. There was no answer.

'Maybe he's already inside,' said Carter.

'Unlikely.'

Seth knocked again. No answer.

He opened the door.

A sickly-sweet odour seeped from around the door as Seth opened it. It turned his stomach, made memories he hoped never to recall come rushing forward. The car stank and it wanted to share the noxious stench with the whole world. The odour was so thick from being contained in such a small area that it would cling to clothes for days.

Carter turned away as if to vomit, but instead pulled a handkerchief from his trouser pocket. He covered his nose and mouth and turned back to do his job. He may have moved more gingerly but at least he was still here.

Maybe he'll make a good partner after all, Seth told himself.

Thomas sat motionless in the driver's seat. His safety belt was fastened, his hands were folded on his lap. His head lolled to one side.

Seth reached in and felt for a pulse. There was none.

'Shit,' he muttered.

Carter reached for his gun. Seth shot him a stern glance.

Carter lowered his hand, sheepishly. 'Sorry. Instinct.'

'It'll get you killed,' said Seth.

He reached around, unfastened the safety belt, and slipped his hand into the dead man's jacket. Thomas's gun was still in its holster. He flicked off the strap that held the gun in place and pulled it out.

'Two bullets missing,' said Seth.

'So he wasn't killed here.'

'Most likely.'

Seth slipped the gun back into its holster and closed the door. 'Let's check inside.'

2

The building had a standard entryway found on all shared accommodation buildings in the area. A simple lock on the door and an intercom so guests could get residents to override the lock. Seth tried the door, found it locked, and pulled a small leather pouch from his coat pocket.

The lock was an old Yale type, probably the same lock that was fitted when the building was new. It provided little resistance to anyone but an honest man. Seth Baron had it open in under a minute. Not bad for someone who only practiced on his desk drawer.

It was cold inside and smelled of mould but at least it was dry. Seth looked around, taking in all the important details quickly. Two doors, both closed, no spy holes. One set of stairs leading up. One set of double doors leading into a communal area of some kind. He turned to Carter and pointed up. The younger man nodded.

They took the stairs one at a time, sticking to the outside, brushing along the wall to minimise the chance of creaking wood giving away their presence. The first floor had four doors leading off from it. All closed, all with spy holes. If anyone was at home, there was a chance they would be seen.

He decided it was a risk worth taking.

They continued up the next flight of stairs, leading to an identical set of four doors. Muted sounds of talking and music came from behind the closest door. Seth pictured the layout of the building in his mind and determined the sounds were coming from the room with the lights he had seen from outside.

Would they be a problem? It was certainly possible, but it was a risk he would have to take.

Carter nodded toward the door, a questioning look on his face. Seth shook his head and pointed upward.

Another flight of stairs, another set of identical doors. Seth looked around. Nobody there. He glanced at Carter, who pointed to the door marked '3c'. Seth nodded and the two men took up positions on either side of the door.

Seth reached out and tried the handle. It turned. He opened

the door gently, pulled his hand back and waited.

Nothing happened.

He looked over at Carter, who shrugged his shoulders.

Seth took a deep breath to calm himself, and stepped inside.

The flat was small, poorly lit and unfurnished. An empty carton of orange juice sat on the counter in the kitchen, beside a tall glass. Seth picked up the glass, sniffed at it, and set it back down on the counter. It smelled of orange but the dried remnants in the bottom were brown.

Carter entered from the hallway. 'There's no one here?' he asked. He kept his voice low.

'There was,' said Seth. He drummed his fingers on the counter. 'Question is: have they left for good?'

'So what do we do?'

'We wait. Maybe she'll come back.'

3

They waited. Outside, rain pattered on the windows. The streets were drenched in water. Seth looked down on the shadowy streets with the people hurrying by, eager to get in out of the rain, and was happy nobody was taking any notice of the car with Thomas' corpse inside. Thank goodness for small mercies.

In the lounge, water leaked in through a damaged seal around the window frame. The flat became icy cold. Seth saw his breath in the air around him.

Good old British craftsmanship, he thought. *They don't make them like they used to*.

23

Carter buttoned up his jacket and stuffed his hands in his pockets. 'Bloody hell. Nobody could live in this place. It's like a fucking freezer.'

'Shh!' hissed Seth.

Footsteps echoed up the stairwell.

Seth crept to the kitchen door and pressed himself up against the wall, hiding as best he could from the view of anyone entering the flat. Carter did the same in the lounge. The flat was a standard sixties design, limiting the options for spaces to hide. Everything was built in right up to the edges, few corners to lurk in, few flat walls to hide against.

A floorboard creaked outside the door to the flat.

The handle clunked, the door cracked open. The men waited, straining to hear and sound.

None came.

They waited. Still nothing.

No choice, Seth thought. *Got to check*.

He risked a glance into the corridor. The door was open, revealing wet footprints on the linoleum in the stairwell. The carpet in the flat was bone dry.

He looked down the corridor toward the lounge, saw Carter staring back at him. Seth motioned toward the stairwell. Carter nodded his assent.

The men crept toward the door, with Seth scanning the area outside. There were footprints outside the door, leading up from the stairs to the left. After that, nothing. The trail seemed to simply end.

Seth stopped at the doorway and looked around. There was no sign of life outside the flat. No noise. No movement.

Nothing. He stepped out into the stairwell and looked around.

A woman was crouched in the corner at the far end of the hallway, by the stairs leading up to the roof. She stared at him, her eyes wide. She looked like a fieldmouse that had been cornered by a cat. Was that genuine fright or an act? Seth could not tell. Best to play it safe.

'Why are you here?' she asked. Her accent was strong, but Seth could not place it. Dutch perhaps, or German.

'I could ask you the same question,' said Seth.

'That's not an answer.'

Seth stepped forward, his hands raised in front of him. 'We're not looking for any trouble. We're here about the warehouse.'

The woman stood up slowly as he approached. She was in her late twenties, medium height, scruffy and malnourished. There were burn marks on her hands and face. Her short, blonde hair was matted and dirty. She stank of stale sweat mixed with a sickly sweet aroma.

Seth remembered that scent well. It had clung to the back of his throat when he had visited the scene of the so-called accident that had killed his son. It had clung to Thomas as he sat in his car outside.

The stench of death. It was an odour that would haunt him for the rest of his life.

'What warehouse?' she asked.

She watched him warily, so ready to move at any indication he was going to get violent that she was practically flinching every time he breathed.

She was ready to bolt at any second. He would have to play this carefully.

Seth stopped walking, but kept his hands raised. 'We just want to know what you were doing there. That's all.'

She pulled her grimy overcoat tightly around herself, hugging it close like it offered some sort of protection. 'None of your business.'

Carter walked up beside Seth. 'Men died there!' he hissed. 'Of course it's our business.'

'Stay back!' she ordered.

'He's right,' said Seth. If this was good cop, bad cop his role was clear. 'We need to know what you were doing there.'

The woman shook her head.

Seth lowered his hands. 'Look, maybe we can make a deal. You tell us what we want to know, and in exchange maybe we can help get you sorted out.'

'I'm fine.'

'You don't look fine,' said Carter.

Seth glanced at the "bad cop". 'Carter, you're not helping.'

'I was just – hey, wait!'

Seth turned back just in time to see a shadow dart across the wall. A metallic echo sounded from the floor above.

'Shit!' Seth shouted as he ran toward the staircase. 'Come on!'

4

The heavy metal door to the roof stood open at the end of a short corridor with bare, grey walls and a dull brown carpet.

Outside, the early morning sunlight was beginning to creep over the horizon. The rain battered the gravel coating the rooftop and pattered on the ceiling of the little stairway exit.

Seth glanced around, saw no sign of the woman, and hurried out onto the roof. Carter lagged behind, out of breath from running up the short flight of stairs.

'Gimme...a minute,' Carter puffed. He leaned against the wall at the top of the stairs. 'I need to catch my breath.'

Seth went on without him. He stepped out into the rain and looked around. The woman was nowhere to be seen.

'Shit,' he muttered.

From the corner of his eye he saw a shadow move. He turned around. There was nothing there.

Behind him, he heard the crunch of wet gravel.

He spun around, ready to catch the woman this time. Something struck him in the chest. He staggered backward, away from the door.

The woman stepped forward, grabbed the door with one hand and slammed it shut. As she took her hand away, a clear bend in the door was visible.

Inside, Carter hammered on the metal. The door did not budge.

'Now we can talk,' said the woman. 'But make it quick.'

Seth straightened his tie, a ploy to buy some time while he got his bearings and assessed the situation. He was on the top of a three-storey building with one exit route, currently blocked by a woman who was clearly fast, strong and in need of a hot bath. His partner was trapped inside, and his other companion was dead in a car.

Had she killed him? Now was the time to find out.

'Why did you kill Thomas?' he asked.

The woman looked at him blankly. 'Thomas who?'

'George Henry Thomas,' said Seth, pointing down at the street. 'The man in car down there.'

'That's nothing to do with me. I haven't a clue who you're talking about.'

Carter hammered on the door. It still would not budge.

'You want me to believe there's a man dead outside the building we know you've been living in, and it's has nothing to do with you being here? That beggars belief.'

'I'm not the only person living here. Now do you have any better questions? I have other things to do, you know.'

'Fine. We'll get the CCTV and find out what happened ourselves.'

'You do that.'

The woman turned to leave.

Seth sighed. 'Gretl, wait.'

The woman stopped, looked around at him. Her heavy woollen coat was soaked with rain. Her hair was matting on her burned face. She did not seem to care.

'What now?' she asked.

'Why are you here?'

She looked at him. Appraising him. Judging his worth, or his combat potential.

'Who are you?' she asked.

'I'm with the Ministry--'

'No,' she said, sharply. 'Who are *you*? Not who are you with.'

'I'm Seth Baron. The man trying to break through the door is Stephen Carter.'

'Baron...' Gretl mused. She chewed her lip as she thought. Seth noticed one of her teeth was pointed, like it was chipped or had lost a cap. She looked up at him suddenly. 'Any relation to Craig Baron?'

'My son,' said Seth.

'I'm sorry for your loss,' she said. She turned to leave.

'I'm sure you are,' Seth sneered. 'Thanks to you his killer will never see justice.'

Gretl turned around slowly. 'It wasn't justice you were looking for.'

'And how the hell would you know? You don't know me.'

'Because I can see it in your eyes. I'm looking for the same thing.'

The woman walked forward. The rain coursing over her was doing nothing to remove the stench that clung to her body like a second skin. She looked him in the eye like she could see into his soul.

'The man who killed your son is still alive. Mark First was not the one who called the hit, he just pulled the trigger. I can help you find the man responsible for your loss.'

'Why would you do that?'

'Because he's working with the man who killed me and my family.'

5

The morning light began to brighten as the Sun rose over

the horizon. Gretl raised her arm to shield her eyes from the onslaught. Seth hardly registered the change, but found the reaction of his quarry intriguing.

'Do you really expect me to believe you're dead?' he asked, matter-of-factly.

Gretl looked at him through eyes that were now barely open, mere slits in puffy, red skin. 'What you think of me is not important. What concerns me is what you want to do about the man who killed your son.'

Seth stared at the woman. She certainly smelled dead, and she seemed to be unconcerned with the open wounds and sores that covered her skin. She was clearly not in complete control of her faculties, so her claims to be deceased could be easily ignored.

But then there was the death certificate; and the newspaper reports, complete with photographs showing a woman who looked exactly like her. Insane or not, those would be difficult to fake. Photoshop was good for forgeries but even forgeries couldn't come direct from the source.

Carter thumped and kicked at the heavy metal door trapping him inside the building. Gretl glanced across at the door, then at the horizon. She looked distinctly ill at ease.

'Something wrong?' asked Seth.

'Make up your mind,' the woman snapped. 'Do you want to deal with the man who killed your son, or do you want to scurry away home?'

Don't rise to her, he told himself. *She's trying to provoke you.*

'Tell me who this man is.'

'*Sollte nicht hier aufgekommen haben*,' Gretl muttered. She turned away and began walking to the edge of the building.

'What?' Seth asked.

She took a deep breath, paused and released it slowly as she looked down at the gravel. 'His name is Allemand. Hans Allemand.'

'I don't recognise the name.'

'There's no reason you should. He works through other people. He stays in the...,' she snapped her fingers a couple of times. 'What is the word? Not scenery. Background? He is hard to find.'

'Which is why you want my help?'

She looked up at him. Seth thought for a moment that there were more sores on her skin now, but dismissed the notion. It was nothing more than his imagination. It couldn't be.

'I did not come here to find you,' she said. 'You came to find me.'

Seth folded his arms. If she didn't want to be here, that was something he could play to his advantage. 'So why are you here?'

'There's no time for this! Maybe later, but not now.'

'Gretl,' Seth said, keeping his voice even but stern. 'Why are you here?'

She sighed and turned away. 'Because Allemand is coming.'

'I meant here as in here, on this rooftop. Why bring me up here when you obviously don't want to be outside?'

She kicked at the gravel. 'Are you going to help me or not?'

'Not unless you tell me what's going on.'

She turned around quickly, her face a picture of anger. 'Fine!' she hissed.

She flipped up the collar on her thoroughly soaked coat. The water on the collar hissed as it came into contact with her skin. Seth noted that she was clearly in pain from the feeling.

'I brought you up here to kill you,' she said. She almost sounded embarrassed. 'You broke into my home, you had a man outside watching me and you wouldn't leave me alone in the corridor. I brought you up here and trapped you so I could kill you then kill your friend. It was the only option.'

Seth's first instinct was to go for his gun and blow the bitch away. He suppressed it for the moment. She was too close and even in pain, he had a feeling she would be too fast for him.

'Why?' he asked, through gritted teeth.

'Because I thought he sent you.'

Seth glanced at the horizon. 'It's going to be dawn any moment.'

Gretl nodded. 'I need to get back inside.'

'I think we need to talk more.'

She shook her head. 'Not out here.'

'Why?'

She pushed up the sleeve on her left arm, revealing bare skin as white as chalk. It began to turn red almost immediately. Blisters arose, turned to sores and wept a deep, red-black puss. 'That's why.'

'Jesus!' said Seth. 'What the fuck?'

Gretl pulled her sleeve back down over the damaged skin.

'If you want to talk, we do it inside.'

6

He could have pushed to stay outside. Some other men would have. Another time, he might have, but not this time. Not when he knew she could easily overpower him even as she bubbled and rotted in front of his eyes. The way her flesh had burned in the sunlight, even the low light of the early dawn; the way that rotten stench had clawed at his lungs, getting worse by the second as the dawn light grew stronger. It churned his stomach he thought he might vomit at any second.

In the end, did he really have a choice? No. Not if he wanted his only lead alive, or whatever she was, and talking to him without the help of a medium. Not if he wanted to know what was going on.

He followed her back inside. She opened the heavy metal door like it was hardly there. He closed it behind them, pulling with all his strength. The hinges were rusted and almost immovable. How much strength was hidden in her gaunt body? She'd done the seemingly impossible right before his eyes.

Carter had pulled his gun on her when she opened the door, but he didn't get the chance to fire. Seth grabbed the weapon as soon as he saw it, twisted the man's hand and disarmed him.

The stupid bastard obviously needed a lot more training.
'She's with me,' said Seth.

33

'What the hell happened?' asked Carter.

'I'll explain in a minute. Follow me.'

They walked down the stairs and back to the empty flat in silence. Questions could wait until they were out of sight of any prying eyes. People would be getting up to go to work within a few hours; chances are some were already up and about. No sense in letting one's self be overheard if you could help it.

Gretl headed straight for the kitchen, pulled a bag from her coat pocket and poured the contents into the glass on the counter. With her back to the door it was hard for Seth to see what exactly she had been carrying.

She picked up the carton of orange juice, shook it and put it down again.

'It's empty,' said Carter, nursing his right shoulder. 'We checked.'

'Pity,' Gretl replied. 'It takes the edge off.'

She sipped at the contents of the glass, keeping her back to the two men.

'Look,' Carter continued. 'Can someone please tell me what's going on here?'

'Ask your boss,' said Gretl. She downed the last of the glass's contents and started to cough. Seth stepped forward to help her. She raised a hand, stopping him. 'I'm fine. Tell your friend why you're here.'

'Not until you explain to me what the fuck happened on the roof.'

She turned and looked at him. Her skin looked smoother, less blemished. The sores were closing, healing, right before his eyes. 'We talked. What more is there to say?'

'Let's start with someone telling me what exactly you are,' said Carter. 'Cause I'm pretty sure dead people don't walk the streets and I've never in my life seen someone go from looking like a disease-ridden tramp to moderately healthy in the blink of an eye.' He grabbed the glass from the woman's hand and sniffed the contents. 'What the hell is this stuff anyway?'

'Blood,' said Gretl. She looked from one man to the other and back again. Her expression was one of confusion. 'Don't you two know anything?'

Carter stared at her, not sure whether to laugh or leave. Seth folded his arms and simply waited for her to continue.

'Look, I thought you were after Allemand. Clearly I was mistaken. So why are you here?'

'Why would we be after Allemand?' asked Seth.

'I asked first.'

Seth shook his head. 'Doesn't work like that. If you want my help, you'll answer my questions.'

'*Got im Himmell*,' Gretl muttered. She ran a hand through her hair. Seth noticed it had grown back and now looked full of vigour. 'He's the head of a cartel that spans Europe, Russia and parts of the Far East. Nasty little shit, too. Works through local crime mobs, keeps out of sight whenever he can. Very hard to track down.'

'And he's coming here?'

'I made sure of it. After the way the meeting at the docks went down, his favourite lap dog is already here. I'll use him to lure him out.'

'So that's why you were down at the warehouse?' asked Carter.

Gretl nodded.

'You upset months of planning for us, you know.'

She shrugged. 'Do I look like I care? I don't even know who you are.' She turned to Seth. 'Are you going to help me or not?'

'You're sure Allemand is the one I should be going after?'

'Dupont is the one who ordered the hit, but he does nothing without Allemand's say so.'

'What are you talking about?' asked Carter.

Gretl ignored him. She kept her eyes on Seth, watching him for any hint of what he was thinking.

You don't get the man who killed him, Seth told himself. *Thanks to this bitch you'll never get the chance. But you can get the man who sent him.*

Is that enough?

He honestly didn't know, but there was only one way to find out.

Seth nodded. Perhaps it was tiredness, or the realisation of what he was getting himself into but he felt every one of his fifty-three years.

'We'll help,' he said. 'But there are conditions.'

Gretl leaned against the counter, appraising her companions, weighing up their strengths and weaknesses in a glance. 'There always are. Name them.'

Chapter Four

1

Jeremy Pellier sat nursing a whisky. Reggie wanted him back in town but he was too drunk to drive. He would get some rest and head back first thing in the morning. A hangover would be the least of his troubles and he knew it all too well, but that problem was hours away.

He downed the whisky and poured himself another. What harm could one more do? He was already three sheets to the wind. Might as well add another sheet while he was at it.

He heard the study door open and turned to see a tall, thin man with thick blonde hair entering. The man closed the door and walked over to where Jeremy was sitting. There were two armchairs by the fire. Jeremy was sat in one of them. The man took the other.

'Who the fuck are you?' Jeremy asked.

'We have a mutual acquaintance,' the man said. His voice carried the subtlest hint of a German accent.

'You obviously didn't hear me. I'll ask again: who the fuck are you?'

'You can call me Hans,' said the man. 'I am told Monsieur Dupont was disappointed by tonight's meeting. I would like to know why.'

'Tough shit. Now get out of my house.'

Hans leaned back in his chair and looked at Jeremy like he was assessing him.

'Mr Pellier,' he said. 'You disappoint me, clinging to these outdated notions. Your house indeed! How can any of us claim ownership of something that may very well stand for longer than we ever could?'

'What the hell are you talking about? Get out, you babbling prick.'

'Possessions, Mr Pellier, are an illusion. We cannot own anything, not one atom. We merely take charge of them for a time; then pass them on when we ourselves pass on.'

'Look, fuck off will you. I'm a busy man.'

Hans leaned forward, resting his forearms on his knees and looking James straight in the eye. James found himself transfixed, unable to tear himself away from the other man's piercing gaze. There was something there, in the back of the man's eyes, that had a dizzying quality; like looking over the edge of the tallest cliff.

'Tell me what happened tonight,' said Hans.

The blonde man's stare burned into James' mind. His eyes prickled, his skin crawled, but he could not turn away.

'Where do you want me to start?' he asked. The words seemed to flow out of his mouth without his mind controlling them.

'Who told the girl we were coming?'

'I don't know.'

'Who is the girl?'

James shook his head, never once averting his gaze from

the other man's stare. 'I don't know.'

'Very well. Who knew about the meeting?'

'Only those who were there,' said James. The words seemed distant, as if heard through cotton wool. He felt as though he was floating a little way behind his body. 'And Reggie.'

'Who is Reggie?'

'Reggie Dixon. He runs the Blexham Green Boys. But he wouldn't rat us out. He had a lot of money resting on this deal.'

'Then why was he not there?'

'He never comes to the deals,' said Jeremy. 'There's too much risk. He could get spotted by the police. Someone could shoot him, like what happened to the others tonight. It's just too much risk.'

Hans leaned forward, resting his forearms on his knees and staring directly into Jeremy's eyes. 'That's not the reason, Mr Pellier. We both know what the true reason is, don't we?'

Jeremy nodded slowly. He did *know* the reason. It was *obvious* to him now. How could he have not realised it sooner?

Hans sat back in his chair and seemed to visibly relax.

The clouds lifted from Jeremy's mind and suddenly he felt more aware of himself. The chair solidified around him, his hands gripping the arms. He felt dizzy and a little sick, like he had just stepped off a fairground ride and was still spinning on the inside.

'What the fuck?' he said. 'What did you fucking do to me?'

'Nothing whatsoever,' said Hans, watching him closely.

'Look, just get the fuck out will you?' Jeremy blustered. 'I'm a busy man.'

Hans nodded. 'Very well.'

He stood and made his way to the door. Jeremy watched him go, flustered and with beads of sweat forming on his brow.

At the doorway, Hans turned and smiled. 'Good night, Mr Pellier. No doubt we will meet again.'

He left, closing the door behind him.

'Not if I see you first,' Jeremy muttered.

2

Jeremy felt like he was floating, detached from everything around him. The world swam around him in a haze of dark clouds and confusion. Somewhere, he could not tell if it was close or afar, a gunshot sounded. He saw flashes of light, shouts and cries, snatches of barked orders. None of it seemed to register fully in his mind.

The girl was there; the one from the meeting. She was fighting someone. Had he also been at the meeting? Was this the meeting, going on right now? He could not be sure. The man pulled a gun, fired at the girl, hit her full in the chest. She staggered backward, almost fell but righted herself at the last moment and lashed out at the man, hitting him square in the face with the palm of her hand. Now he staggered backward, lost his footing and fell.

The girl dropped down on top of him, landing with her knee on his chest. Jeremy heard a cry of pain. Was it from the man? He could not tell. It did not matter. In Jeremy's mind, none of what he was seeing or hearing mattered. The man on the ground lashed out with his fists, sometimes connecting with the girl, sometimes not. She did not seem to care.

She reached out with both hands, took hold of the man's head and twisted.

Now Jeremy was looking up at the girl, seeing her in detail for the first time. She was attractive, but it was not her looks that made her so. She looked plain, the kind of girl he wouldn't give a moment's thought to if he passed her in the street. But there was something about her, something that held his attention. He couldn't put his finger on it.

She took her hands off him and stood up. He could not breathe. He could not move. His throat tightened as he gasped for breath that would not come. He could feel his mind going cold and numb. His body felt like it was no longer part of him. It was lost in a sea of numbness. The bitch had broken his neck! He was going to die, and she was the one that had killed him.

She walked away, and he saw she was no longer the girl from the meeting. Now he looked more closely, he could not believe he had thought she was a girl at all. It was Reggie. Reggie had done this to him. The old bastard! He'd set this whole meeting up to get rid of Jeremy and his men.

The world lost focus. Once again, Jeremy was floating in the cloudy realm where nothing was real. His mind burned with rage. He thought he could trust that old bastard but he had been wrong. Now Reggie was going to pay.

41

He woke in a cold sweat, sitting in the leather chair by a fire that was no more than barely glowing embers now. The whisky glass was still in his hand. He looked at it like it was alien to him.

'Then why was he not there?'

The German's words echoed in his mind. How had he known? Who could say.

All that mattered right now was that Reggie Dixon was going to pay for what he had done tonight. Good men, loyal men, had died because that old shit had ratted them out.

He would pay dearly.

Chapter Five

1

Carter paced back and forth in front of a large window overlooking the street. He was flicking through a grey file, one of a seemingly endless number of similar files Seth had until now kept locked in the drawers of his office cabinet. The old man had been working on this case for far too long, and from the look of some of the documents he was reading, cuttings from newspapers from all around the world, he had not been working alone.

He finished reading an article about a serial killer in Adelaide in the 1920s and looked over at Seth. He was sitting at his desk, pecking at his keyboard with two fingers. He had been working here for longer than Carter had been out of school and yet the guy had never found time to learn to use a computer.

Seth looked over at him. 'Seen enough?'

'I don't know,' said Carter. 'It's hard to believe one guy is responsible for all this. It goes back decades.'

'You saw Gretl. How do you explain her?'

Carter looked at the older man. 'You think she's a...hell, I don't even know what to call her.'

Seth began tap-tapping on the keyboard. 'I think she's a

vampire.'

'No way,' Carter snorted. 'No fucking way.'

'I saw her skin burn up in the sunlight. She started to look normal after drinking blood. Her death certificate is sat on my desk. What more proof do you want?'

'I saw a kid with a sunlight allergy on the television once.'

Seth looked up from the computer. 'Did she drink blood?'

'You can't honestly think that was real.'

'Why not? What else was it?'

'It could have been anything! The girl's clearly a fucking loon!'

Seth turned back to the computer. 'Keep reading.'

'Why? What am I going to find?'

'Enough evidence to make you change your assumptions about the world.'

Carter turned toward the window and looked out at the late afternoon skyline. There were dark clouds on the horizon and there was a chill in the air already. The night was going to be long, cold and unwelcoming. Just what he did not need.

2

Carter sat in the passenger seat of Seth's 1993 Volvo, a car that had once been a deep blue colour and was now a deep rust. He was reading yet another file. The cover was grey, like the others. The contents were horrible.

Photographs from Paris, Bonn, Luxembourg and Monaco. Anywhere this Allemand person had been spotted, horrible crimes were recorded and, once cameras were part of the equipment police used on their cases, photographs had been taken. Before that, it was all sketches from local people who were drafted in to record the scene by morbid collectors of gruesome tales; or just plain old witness descriptions.

He turned to another file. This one was marked KC3.

'What's KC3 stand for?' he asked.

'You don't need to know,' said Seth.

'So I'm cleared to read files mentioning it, but not to know what it stands for?'

'That's right.'

Carter shrugged. It was not the first time he had come across something immensely stupid during his time at the Ministry and he doubted it would be the last. The higher-ups liked to play at being spies, he decided.

Let them play while we're out here, getting our throats cut by people who drink blood. Just let me get home in one piece.

He opened the next file and started to read. It was information on a network of dealers in occult items, highly restricted artefacts and information. The file suggested Allemand was not just involved with the network but may in fact be a major, if not the sole, driving force behind it all.

'So he's here because of this occult smuggling ring?' asked Carter.

Seth nodded, took a sip of coffee from his flask. 'It looks that way.'

'And he's using a network of drug dealers to move the artefacts? He's hiding contraband behind more contraband.'

'You've got to give him credit,' said Seth. 'He knows how to make the most of what he has.'

'This is bloody stupid,' said Carter. He dropped the file on his lap and pulled a packet of cigarettes out of his pocket.

'Stupid?' asked Seth. 'This guy has operated almost without detection for longer than we can possibly know. He's practically got the whole of Europe working for him in some regard. He's vicious, devious and knows how to make sure his dealings stay out of sight and all you have to say about him is he's stupid?'

'I didn't say he was stupid. I said this is stupid. This, right here. Us sitting in this car, waiting for a woman who we can't shine a torch on in case she accidentally explodes to come and talk to us about fighting the King of the fucking world.'

Seth sighed. 'She won't explode.'

'What?'

'You can shine your torch on her. She won't explode. That's not how it works.'

'So how does it work?'

'I don't know. I'm not a scientist but I'm pretty sure she won't just blow up under any old light.'

'It would make our job easier if she did,' said Carter. He lit his cigarette, took a long, draw; savouring the taste. 'Then we could just get his Allemand guy to meet us at the stadium. Turn on the floodlights and the fucker would go up like an oily rag.'

'There she is,' said Seth. He twisted the cap back on his flask and shoved it into the webbing on the back of the passenger-side seat.

A woman approached, walking down the path next to the road. She was wearing the exact same clothes as she had been wearing the night before. When she neared the car, she nodded at the two men sat inside, and headed into a nearby all-night café.

Seth waited five minutes, then he and Carter followed her inside. They found her sitting at a small, round table at the back of the café, with a small cup of coffee in front of her. She showed no sign of emotion as the two men sat down around the table.

She sipped her coffee and watched Seth. Her face bore a world-weary expression that he not only fully understood but also shared on occasion. She was tired of life, and wanted the task they all now shared over with so she could move on. He could understand that. He had brooded over the death of his son for far less time than she had been chasing her target and already he was suffering from the strain of the ordeal.

She took another sip of her coffee, set the cup down on the table and sighed. Seth looked at the cup with an expression bordering on amazement. *So vampires can drink things other than blood*, he thought. *Another way to identify them crossed off the list, then.*

'So...,' said Carter.

Seth glanced at his partner. He seemed ill at ease this close to his first undead. Clearly the Ministry was not doing enough to train its people any more.

'You wanted to talk,' said the vampire. 'So talk. I don't have all night.'

'Let's get the conditions of our working together sorted out before we go any further,' said Seth. 'You and I both want to know the limits here, don't we? There's a lot at risk.'

'You already know my rules. I'm after the German. When I catch him, he's mine. Don't interfere with any of that and we'll get along fine.'

'Very well,' said Seth. He noted her care to not mention names. Perhaps she was not as amateur as he had given her credit for. 'We can accept that. Let me tell you my conditions.'

'Go ahead.'

'Condition one: we share everything. No secrets, no pieces of information left out because you think it's not relevant. If you find something out, I want to know about it.'

'Very well. Is that all?'

'Not quite. We've been tracking the people "the German" has involved in this operation for a long time. We have a good idea how they operate and how they will react to a given situation. That means we only move in when I am sure we can get the result we want.'

'So you want me to hold off until you give the go-ahead,' she said flatly.

'Yes.'

She sighed. 'I've been tracking him for almost fifty years. I've more experience "in the field", as you call it, than both of you combined. Do not act like I am an amateur who will mess up your precious operation or we will part company.'

Gretl locked eyes with Seth as she spoke. They stared at one-another while Carter looked back and forth between them.

What is Baron thinking? Carter asked himself. He may have been new to the idea that vampires existed but even he knew that looking into a vampire's eyes could put you under their control. Seth was taking a hell of a risk.

Seth's gaze broke first. He looked away, visibly angry with himself. 'Fine. I apologise for the insult but I have to insist that we make the call on when to go in. It's our assets that are on the line here, not yours.'

Gretl took another sip of her coffee as she considered the proposal. Carter wondered whether vampires had to throw up what they ate and drank, or whether they could actually process food like a normal person. He decided not to risk asking about it.

'Very well,' said Gretl.

'Excellent. Now let's share what we know about the German and his plans, so we can all get up to speed. Carter, get the coffees in.'

Chapter Six

1

'Mister Pellier,' said Allemand. 'It should be clear to a man of your stature that the current bosses of this town are not long for this world. They grow old. They grow weak. They must be removed quickly and cleanly before an ill-thought-out power grab fractures the delicate empires they have constructed.'

Allemand sat in a leather chair by the fire, his legs stretched out in front of him, crossed at the ankles. He held a brandy glass in the palm of his right hand and swirled the liquid around the bottom of the glass' wide base like an expert.

Pellier felt the man was making himself far too comfortable in his home but there was a strange compulsion at the back of his mind to keep the man happy and allow him to stay as long as he wished.

He is doing me no harm. He is doing good by me. I need him.

He had never had to think about that with Reggie Dixon. Dixon wore his heart on his sleeve. This man, this new boss, hid far too much.

He walked to the bar, poured himself another drink and

returned to the vacant chair by the fire. The German man smiled a thin smile at him and raised his glass. Pellier raised his glass also.

'To a successful future,' said Allemand.

'To a successful future.'

Pellier downed his drink. Allemand continued to swirl his in the glass, not touching a drop.

'What is it you need from me exactly?'

'I want you to run this city for me. I have shipments coming in from all over the world, so I need to keep moving around. I need someone I can trust here in town to make sure my operations are concluded without a problem.'

'And Mr Dixon can't do that for you?'

'Herr Dixon and I do not see eye to eye,' said Allemand. His accent was stronger when he was annoyed, Pellier noticed. 'He will be a thorn in my side if not removed. You will remove him for me and in exchange, you get to run the city - the entire city - in his place.'

Pellier's mind was still clouded on the issue of Reggie Dixon and what he meant but even in the depths of uncertainty he knew one thing. The old bastard needed to pay for his betrayal at the last meeting. Men had died, so it was only fitting that he died as a result. If that meant Pellier took over in his place, then that was just the icing on the cake.

2

Allemand left Pellier's pretentious little house in his equally

Zoë Robinson

pretentious black Mercedes at four in the morning, looking
well fed and so damn sure of himself that Gretl Lune wanted
to rush over and beat the smile of his smug face there and
then.

Instead she chose to stay crouched low in the trees on the
opposite side of the road, watching the bastard and keeping
an eye on the house as well, in case any more bastards
came seeping out.

Allemand got into his car and drove away. It hurt Gretl like
a knife to the gut to watch him simply drive away but she had
no car of her own that night and had no chance of keeping
up with him on foot, so she had to swallow her hurt and keep
hidden until he was out of sight.

Tonight, the collaborator in the house was the target. She
would make Pellier talk if it was the last thing she did.

She checked the area, made certain that there was nobody
around to see what she was about to do, then crossed the
road quickly and confidently. The key to not being noticed
was to look like you were acting naturally and that you were
supposed to be doing whatever you were about to do.

The driveway up to the house was short and covered in tiny
white pieces of gravel; the kind of gravel that was not native
to the area. It had to be shipped in specially to line
driveways. What pretentious nonsense.

Pretentious or not, it would make a crunching sound if she
stood on it. She could be as quiet as the night if she wanted
to be, but she could not change the fact that walking on
gravel would give away her position if Pellier was still awake.

She made for the low stone wall to the right of the drive and

52

vaulted it in one swift movement, dropping into a crouch on the grass on the other side. From there she could creep up to the house while hugging the shadows, remaining unseen until it was time to strike.

The side door to the house was clearly alarmed, as were all the windows on the ground floor. There was a window on the first floor that was slightly open. It had frosted glass, suggesting it was a bathroom. The porch roof stood below it. Perfect.

She walked to the side of the porch, checking the area for signs of life as she did so. Nobody about. Excellent. She scanned the doors and windows around the porch. Lights off, nobody visible behind the windows. The probability was high that there was no one around to see her. Just as she liked it.

Gretl leapt directly upward, caught the side of the porch roof with her hands and swung forward to gain enough momentum to help pull herself onto the roof. The tiles were slippy under her hands and feet, a vestige of the rain from earlier that day. She paid extra attention to her footing and her balance in case the moisture made her fall.

She crept across the roof to the window, trying her best to keep as silent as possible. With both hands, she grabbed the window and tugged it open. Speed was essential here. If the window was alarmed, it would be set off whether she opened it slowly or not, so it was best to get it open all the way quickly, then get inside.

She slithered into the bathroom, over the windowsill and down onto the tiled floor. Moving like a snake, she had been almost soundless.

Chalk up another "vampire factoid" to the realm of superstition. Invitations were not, and had never been, necessary for this predator to attack you in your home.

3

Jeremy Pellier sat by the fire, watching the last of the coal glowing red in the grate and wondering what he would do once he ruled the city. He would not make any major changes at first, that would only serve to make people nervous of him. He wanted the transition to go as smoothly as possible.

The door creaked behind him. Before he could turn around fully, a knife was at his throat.

'Don't move,' said Gretl.

'What the fuck is this, foreigners night?' asked Pellier.

Gretl had to give the man points for not being scared. She had been scared when her home had been invaded back in the sixties. Having said that, she had never been a hardened thug; so maybe home invasions were an occupational hazard one just had to get used to.

'Look at me,' she commanded.

Pellier turned around slowly. His eyes scanner her athletic frame, starting at the hips and working upward. The stupid grin that developed on his thin mouth disappeared almost as soon as his eyes met hers. He had been placed under the spell of another vampire, and very recently. Gretl fought to penetrate Allemand's barriers. The old German bastard was strong, but not as strong in the mental skills as she was. *Thank fuck for that*, she told herself.

'Tell me what Allemand has planned for you,' she commanded.

Pellier told her everything. From their first meeting to their latest just that evening. He told her of the plans for a second meeting; explained their goal of their ruling the city through a combined will; and how Pellier would act as an intermediary for his master once the city was under their control.

When Gretl left, Pellier did not even remember she had been there.

4

'Baron, when you get this tell your men to get ready,' said Gretl. She was walking down a quiet road with a mobile phone she had taken from a would-be mugger held to her ear.

'Pellier talked. Allemand is planning to try for another deal in three days' time. I've left a package for you at your office. Don't try to call me on this number. I'm disposing of the phone when I hang up.'

She hung up, wiped her mouth more out of habit than from fear of there being any trace of blood on her face, and tossed the mobile into the river. Then she headed to the nearest boarded-up house, forced her way inside and settled down to another long day of restless sleep while waiting for darkness.

Chapter Seven

1

'Condition one,' Seth had said over a cup of hot coffee in one of the greasiest cafés he had ever sat in. 'We share everything. No secrets. If you find something out, I want to know about it.'

He had not expected her to provide so much so quickly.

Hand-written notes, scrawled on scraps of paper in the most illegible writing he had ever seen, all now scattered over his desk.

She must have been collecting this crap for years and now all he had to do was write it up in a decent form; then cross-reference it with everything the Ministry had in its computers. That would take days, but after a lifetime in the civil service, he could handle the waiting. It was a necessary evil when it came to being part of the bureaucratic machine. Besides, he had people to do it for him if he really wanted it done quickly.

He had chosen to type it all up personally, so he had a chance to read everything as it was going in. It would take all day to sort out the scraps of paper and put them into a coherent order before he could start typing them up, but there was nothing more important to do.

He finished typing the last sentence of a file on Allemand's movements in the 1980s. Places he had lived, people he had worked with. Some of this tied in with investigations Seth had run years earlier, but he had never heard of Allemand before.

'He works through intermediaries,' she had told him. 'Don't expect to turn up anything on him directly.'

He was chasing a ghost on the word of a woman who stank like a latrine and whose skin fell off in bright light. He was taking a lot on faith, that much was certain.

She didn't smell after she drank blood, he thought. What other surprises is she hiding? *Do all vampires rot when they don't drink?*

Carter burst into the office, carrying a file in one hand and a coffee in the other.

'Got him,' he said, dropping the file onto the desk and jabbing at a photograph with his free hand.

'Who?'

'Allemand. He's a sneaky fucker but I knew he couldn't hide forever.'

Seth looked at the photograph. It was in a newspaper clipping from a French newspaper in the late 1960s. In the background of a picture showing the aftermath of a car accident was a tall, thin man with light coloured hair and a beard. The printing was too low quality to give any more information.

'What makes you think it's him?' Seth asked.

Carter handed him a printout of a photograph. 'I found this on a website charting the history of the Scholz family in Munich.'

'Who are they?'

'Nobody important, until you see him.' Carter pointed to a young man, the eldest son of the family. 'This was taken around 1901, before the family were called Scholz. The young lad there is called Hans Allemand.'

'So what happened to him?'

'Apparently he went off to fight in the first world war and never came back.'

Seth stared at the photograph. The boy could not have been more than thirteen when the picture was taken.

He handed the photograph back. 'It's a start. See what else you can find out about him.'

2

Gretl sat on the roof of the Victoria, a pseudo-Victorian building in the centre of town. It had been a theatre in the 1960s, a cinema in the 1980s and was now a trendy wine bar on the ground floor with a cheap and nasty nightclub occupying the two floors above it. If there was anywhere to pick up scum in this town, the nightclub in the Victoria was the place.

The night was still young and she had barely woken but already the craving was threatening to overwhelm her. She had been hooked on cigarettes when she died and the need for nicotine had been tremendous. Her body ached, her mind pulsed with every heartbeat and she felt herself become so tense whenever she could not get one more draw on those little white sticks.

She experienced the effects of withdrawal whenever it was a choice between cigarettes or little Claus having a new pair of shoes; or the right books for school; or any one of a hundred other things a growing child needs. Money had been tight, but she could always fight the cravings when things got too bad.

She would give anything to feel those cravings now. Compared to the hell she faced each night, they were paradise.

She scanned the crowds that were starting to form outside the more popular pubs and clubs. Somewhere in each crowd there was a target. She just needed to find one. Which unlucky sod would it be tonight?

Outside the Victoria, a man in a white tracksuit sauntered over to a blue Fiat, looked both ways, then leaned into the passenger-side front window. Gretl watched him talking to the driver; saw him pass something over to him and receive something in return. Then he stood up, patted the roof and walked away.

Dealer, she thought, keeping her eyes on the car. *Perfect*.

3

'Allo there, darlin',' the dealer grinned. His smile was crooked, like he's taken one too many punches to his already less than perfect face while growing up. 'What can I do for you?'

His eyes flicked up from her chest for a brief second, meeting hers. It was all she needed. His vision glazed, his jaw sagged in the vacant way that told her he would do anything she asked.

She smiled. 'Let's go for a ride.'

She slipped into the passenger seat. He started the car and headed out of town.

Gretl had spent the last few decades of her post-mortem existence perfecting the art of keeping people under her control. At the start, it had been necessary to make sure she could get a full day's rest without being disturbed. Later on, she had tried to develop something of a spy network to track Allemand's movements across the continent. Now she had reached that point in her career as a puppet master that she could hook a man and have him dance to her tune without the need to maintain constant eye contact.

Few monsters ever got to that level; most were killed by the people they practiced on. She had been lucky in that respect.

Gretl looked around the car as they drove, taking in the black jacket slung on the back seat and bulge in the dealer's trouser pocket. Either money or drugs. She hoped it was money, drugs were useless to her.

'Stop here,' she said.

The dealer pulled over to the side of the road and stopped the car.

She leaned over toward him, put her hands on his shoulders and whispered in his ear. 'Sleep.'

He closed his eyes and went limp, his head falling forward. She pushed it to one side and bit down hard on his neck. The blood flowed slowly, but it was warm and the pleasure centre of her brain stepped into overdrive as the sharp, iron taste flowed over her tongue. Her heart raced, her pupils dilated. She sucked at the wound, gulping the warm, red liquid as fast as she could. She had to get as much out as possible before the wound clotted. It was a personal rule; one bite per victim. Any more and she risked killing the poor sap.

Whether the victim was a dealer or a saint, she did not kill. She was not a murderer. Killing was Allemand's territory. Despite everything he had taken from her, she still had her conscience.

The blood stopped. She licked sorrowfully at the young man's neck, savouring the last of his precious, life-giving fluid, then slumped back in her seat and let it work its magic on her. The wounds that had not healed the night before closed, leaving no trace. She looked whole again. Human. The spectre of death lifted.

Her main business concluded, she searched the man's pockets, finding a roll of twenties, a half-empty packet of cigarettes and a Bic lighter. She took them all, pulled him out of the car and drove back into town.

4

Gretl pulled up in the car park outside a large supermarket and finished her cigarette as she watched people going in and out of the giant building. She needed a change of clothes after last night's escapades and in the early evening, most shops were closed. This place sold clothes that looked cheap but at least she would not stand out amongst the regular crowds. It would do, for now.

She tossed the cigarette butt out of the car window, checked herself in the passenger side mirror, and climbed out of the car.

Being able to check her appearance in a mirror had seemed strange at first. When she had first clawed her way out of a shallow grave back in the 1960s, she had at first been shocked by the fact that vampires actually existed; then further shocked that many of the common ideas about vampires were totally untrue.

What was true and what was not seemed arbitrary to her, but she had committed them to memory nevertheless. It was always good to know your own strengths and weaknesses, especially when you were dealing with a campaign to exact revenge on someone with the same powers as yourself.

No reflection in mirrors? That was a lie. Sunlight can kill you? That was unfortunately true, but the mechanism was more horrible than story books and Hollywood had imagined. No vampire burst into flames or turned to dust in sunlight, no matter how old it was. Instead, they rotted - and quickly. It was amazing just how soon flesh could turn to foetid stench, pustules and necrotic fluids of green and black.

The first time she had seen that happen, she had vomited. Vampires could eat and drink, that was another thing Hollywood often got wrong.

5

The choice of clothes was surprisingly large and the quality was better quality than she had expected. She selected three black trouser suits; blouses in a variety of colours; and two pairs of decent, black shoes with low heels. The idea was to look like she was an average office worker; the kind of person one would not think was out of place where she would be hanging around for the next few days, or possibly weeks if things did not quite go to plan. If she wanted to look like a street urchin or a student, her current clothing would serve perfectly well.

With her outfits chosen, she headed for the hair and makeup aisle and bought tanning lotion, makeup to suit a darker complexion and hair dye in as natural a red as she could find. She passed by the optician then stopped, turned around and headed back. She had never needed spectacles but they helped change the face enough that anyone not paying real attention might mistake her for someone else. Every little helped.

On her way to the checkout, she picked up more orange juice.

6

Jeremy sat in the King's Arms, nursing a pint of Sovereign ale and waiting for Reggie to show his face. He had been there for almost twenty minutes, which was par for the course for the old bastard, but tonight he was not in the mood to be messed around. If he didn't turn up in the next ten minutes, there would be hell to pay.

'Jeremy my old son,' Reggie called from across the room. 'It's good to see you looking so well.'

'I've been better,' said Jeremy. 'What did you want to see me about.'

Reggie took a seat across the table from Jeremy and leaned in close. Horton, his stocky minder took up position watching the crowd.

'Someone set us up last night,' said Reggie. 'And I think I know who.'

Yeah, I bet you fucking do, thought Jeremy. 'Oh yeah?' he said.

'There's a guy in Broughton called Simon Trafford. You know him?'

'Can't say I do.'

'No, I thought not. He's small time, but the word is that he makes a little on the side as a police informer. I've had my suspicions about the little shit for a while now, and recently he's been good for me. I've got him telling the rozzers what I want them to know and all that.'

'What's this got to do with last night?'

'Hold your horses, old son. I'm just getting to that.' He nodded to Horton, who passed an envelope to Jeremy. 'That was on my desk this morning.'

Jeremy opened the envelope and pulled out two photographs. Both showed a middle aged man with receding hair and very little chin talking to a short woman in a long coat.

'I assume this bloke is Trafford,' said Jeremy. 'The woman looks like the bitch from last night.'

'Right on both counts.'

'So what do you want from me?'

'Isn't it obvious? These two wronged us last night, old son, and if we are wronged, should we not be avenged?'

Reggie stood up and made to leave. 'Give me a call when this is sorted out.'

Jeremy looked at the photographs again. This made no sense to him. Reggie had been the setup merchant. He had seen that, had he not? So what was this?

Are these photos real? Are they from before the deal got busted, or more recent? Is this another of Reggies setups?

How can I find out the truth?

He downed his pint, stuffed the photographs and the envelope in his pocket and headed out into the street. He needed to think this over.

7

Gretl rinsed her hair with the shower attachment fitted over the bath, leaning over the side in a most undignified and uncomfortable position as she did so. She wondered why so many women felt the need to go through this process regularly. It made no sense to her. Such a rigmarole for little real gain. If she had no pressing need to change her appearance after the fight at the warehouse, she would never in a million years want to have to waste time on this.

Still, it beats the old methods, she thought. At least now it's just a case of rinse, soak, rinse.

She squeezed as much water out of her hair as she could,

grabbed an old towel and dried herself off. Her hair was still damp but that was fine. She looked at herself in the mirror, making sure she had covered every patch of hair she could see, picked up a pair of scissors and began cutting her hair into a short, spiky style. It would not look great since she was doing it herself, but it would be passable and that was all she needed for now.

There was only one thing left to do: fake tan. She had not been looking forward to that; it was even more hassle and undignified posturing than the hair dye.

It can wait until the hair is dry and I've had a cigarette, she decided.

Chapter Eight

1

'I don't see her,' said Carter. 'Think she's actually going to come?'

Seth kept his eyes on the street ahead. The rain had eased off during the afternoon but showed no signs of abating entirely. 'Of course she'll come. She wants this just as much as we do.'

They sat in Seth's black sedan and waited, watching the rain fall and the pedestrians hurry down the road in the hope of getting out of the weather quickly.

The minutes dragged by and Seth was beginning to give up hope when he spotted a redhead in black-rimmed glasses walking toward the car. It took him a moment to recognise her, but he did. All his training coupled with years of on-the-streets experience had made him an expert in recognising people.

It had been three days since they had met in person but she was still fresh in his memory thanks to spending days analysing photographs and other records. Her hair might be different and her spectacles changed the eye-to-face ratio slightly, but her overall face shape was the same. She may be able to fool the average person with her disguises, but he was not having any of it.

He unlocked the car doors and she climbed into the back.

'We were starting to think you weren't coming,' he said.

'I got delayed. Let's not hang around here. You were easy to spot; chances are I'm not the only one who saw you.'

Seth turned the ignition, pulled out into the road and headed off at a steady twenty miles per hour. There was no sense drawing attention to them by speeding.

'What was the delay?' asked Carter.

'It doesn't matter,' Gretl replied, sounding edgy. 'It won't affect tonight.'

Seth hoped Carter knew better than to push for more information. He glanced in the rear-view mirror, noted the vampire's smarter appearance: black suit, black blouse; all neat and ironed. She had even brushed her hair. Maybe she had been telling the truth about how important tonight was to her.

'So what have you found out?' Gretl asked.

'Dupont is meeting with Reggie Dixon again tonight. They're trying for another deal,' said Seth. 'What about you?'

'Allemand will be there too. So will his new lackey.'

'What new lackey?' asked Carter. 'Why didn't we hear about this?'

'His name is Pellier,' said Gretl. She pronounced the name in what sounded like a flawless French accent. 'He's been sniffing around town, asking about me for the last couple of days. I just found out tonight that he's working with Allemand.'

'If that's true, tonight is going to be more complicated than I thought,' Seth said.

'It doesn't change the plan.' Gretl's tone was firm. 'Everyone we want is going to be at the meeting tonight. If we're going to hit them, this is the time to do it. The last thing we need is to give them time to work out what's happening and go to ground. Agreed?'

'Agreed,' said Seth.

'Then let's get our gear ready and get in there.'

2

Jeremy Pellier pulled up behind the deep blue Mercedes and climbed out, turning up the collar on his jacket and wishing the rain would ease up for a while, give everyone a break and a chance to dry off a little. He hated weather like this. Why he had ever come back from France was a mystery right now. Better weather, cheaper food, good drink. Oh, how he wished he was back there instead of being here in this cold, wet, miserable country.

The rear door on the Mercedes opened with a clunk. He rushed over and climbed inside.

'Jesus, it's wet out there,' he said. He could feel himself shaking and tried to convince himself that it was just because of the cold. An attack of the nerves would not be a good thing right now.

The man in the driver's seat passed a plastic bag over his shoulder to Jeremy. 'You'll be needing this.'

Jeremy looked in the bag. Inside was a 9mm Glock; several rounds of ammunition in black clips; and one tarnished silver clip.

'Remember our agreement,' said the driver.

'Yeah.' Jeremy's voice was flat, betraying no emotion. 'I remember.'

He slipped the bag under his jacket, stepped out of the Mercedes and headed back to his Toyota.

By the time he had fastened his seat belt, the other car was gone.

3

Gretl had set herself up in the video room of the factory whose yard was to be the meeting place for that night's deal. Getting in had not been a problem. She vaulted the rear wall of the warehouse next door, climbed its fire escape and jumped onto the factory roof, then let herself in through an access point put there to make maintenance of the factory's flat roof easier. Now the guards were unconscious in a corner and she was sat in front of a bank of monitors. She pulled the bluetooth earpiece out of her pocket and fastened it to her ear. It felt uncomfortable; she imagined people would get used to them if they used them enough but she hated it, always would.

'I'm in,' she said.

'Good,' said Seth through the earpiece. His voice was crackled with a little static but the message came through clear enough for her to understand him. 'We're almost in position. Keep this channel open.'

'Will do.'

She sat back in the chair and waited. It was up to the

enemy to make their move now. All she could do was wait.

4

Seth watched as his men took up position on the roof of the factory across from the target; in the café down the road and in vans parked at several key points down the road. When the time came, they would be able to block off the street quickly and take out anyone who tried to resist arrest.

Carter fidgeted in his seat. The younger man was poor company on a job like this. Seth's usual manner of working was to relax into an almost meditative state; clear of mind but alert enough to respond quickly when the time came. Carter's incessant fidgeting and impatience ruined all that.

'How long do you think we've got to wait?' Carter asked.

'Half an hour, maybe more,' Seth replied curtly.

'Time enough for a brew, then.' Carter unbuckled his seat belt. 'Want one?'

Seth sighed, squeezed the bridge of his nose. It had been a long day. Maybe a cup of tea was not a bad idea. 'Sure. Black, no sugar.'

As he waited for his tea, Seth settled into stakeout mode. He sat impassively, breathing slowly, watching the world go by. A cat walked along the high wall surrounding the factory. It reminded him of Tom; the cat he had had as a child. He put the memory aside for now, not wanting any distractions. A man walking a German shepherd passed him without a second glance. Seth watched the man in the rear view mirror as he walked his dog down the street, in case he was a lookout for the targets. The man turned a corner into a housing estate and disappeared. Probably just some guy out walking his dog, Seth decided. He gave him no more thought.

Carter climbed back into the car, a cardboard drinks carrier in one hand and a paper bag in the other. He passed a cup to Seth and proffered the bag. 'Doughnut?'

Seth took the cup but declined the food, as tempting as it looked. 'I'm coeliac.'

'Shit, sorry. I forgot.'

'It's okay. What did the guys in the café have to say.'

'They've seen nothing so far. They'll radio if anything comes up.'

Seth nodded. 'It's early yet.'

They sat in silence, sipping over-hot tea and waiting. Time lost its meaning as Seth slipped further into stakeout mode until suddenly a voice came over the radio.

'Black Mercedes approaching,' said Porter. 'Plates registered to a van reported stolen two months ago. Two occupants. Passenger matches the description of Hans Allemand.'

Seth turned on the microphone on his lapel. 'Roger that. Hold position until my signal. Let's see what he does.'

The Mercedes rolled into view at a leisurely pace, keeping just under the speed limit. It passed the factory gates and headed on down the road. Seth watched it go by, the streetlights making it difficult to make out the people inside the vehicle. A drive-by inspection of the area before starting business was not unexpected under the circumstances.

Gretl's voice crackled over the radio. 'Baron, the target is here.'

'I know,' Seth replied. 'We just saw him go past.'

'No, I mean he's here. In the factory.'

That was quick, Seth thought. Out loud he asked 'How did he get inside? He was in the car just a second ago.'

'Did you see him?'

'The spotters ID'd him.'

'Did *you* see him?'

Seth thought back to the car and how the light had shone off the windows. 'No.'

'We can move fast. Faster than you can follow. Bear that in mind tonight.'

Seth went quiet. If Allemand could move that fast, could any of his men, all normal human beings, stand a chance?

Carter's voice brought him back to he present. 'If he's in the factory, do you think he suspects something?'

'It's unlikely,' said Gretl. 'It looks like he's finding somewhere to hide.'

'Come again?' asked Seth.

Gretl did not reply right away. When she did, her voice was distant, like the radio was a secondary concern and she was paying more attention to something else. 'There's more going on here than we thought. Stay where you are for now.'

'I don't think that's an option,' said Seth, readying his weapon. 'The bad guys are on their way in.'

Chapter Nine

1

After the first target arrived, time passed so slowly Seth could almost imagine he felt his fingernails growing. This was the worst part of any job; knowing something is going to happen but being unable to interfere lest you make it worse, or stop it happening altogether. They had to hold off until the purpose of the meeting was established, and it became clear just what kind of crime was being committed. Without that, it was just some guys they had next to nothing by way of evidence on, having a meeting. They were powerless to act.

The next car arrived twenty minutes later, amidst radio silence. Seth watched the silver Toyota pull into the yard and four men climb out. He did not recognise them immediately, but Carter did.

'That's Dupont,' he said. 'The one in the blue suit.'

Seth sipped his tea. The lukewarm liquid coated his dry throat, seeping its way through tensed muscles.

Dupont. The man who had ordered the hit on his son. He would be his priority.

2

Gretl scoured the screens before her, searching for any clue about what Allemand intended to do. The old man was hiding the shadows between two storage tanks, near enough that he would be able to see and hear everything that happened at the meet, but far enough away that anyone in the yard would never spot him. He stood motionless, a feat rarely achieved by mortal and immortal men alike. She wondered how long he had practiced.

The radio crackled. She ignored it; paranoid that the moment she turned away from the screens, Allemand would disappear. She had come too close to let him slip away now.

'Black Mercedes on Woodrow Lane, heading to junction with Strathclyde Road,' said the radio.

Another voice crackled over the channel. She did not recognise it. 'Any word on the occupants?'

'Three men,' said the first voice. 'Looks like Dixon and Pellier in the back. Unknown male driving.'

'Here we go,' Gretl told herself. Leaning forward, her head almost pressed up against the largest of the monitors, her eyes fixed on Allemand. 'Let's see you get out of this one, you bastard.'

3

'We should be there in a minute, sir,' said the driver.

Reggie Dixon said nothing. Jeremy Pellier shifted uncomfortably in his seat. The gun the German had given him was taped uncomfortably to his thigh, hidden under his trousers but still conspicuous in how it made him walk. He wanted this over with quickly before anyone spotted anything amiss.

'When we get there, you keep close to me,' said Reggie. 'I don't trust this French tosser to play straight, so when he makes his move, I want you there to deal with 'im, got it?'

'Got it,' said Jeremy. God, he wanted this night over with.

The car pulled into the yard. There were two other cars already parked there, at the back; cutting off a clear run into the building. That was okay by Jeremy. What he wanted was a clear run out of the yard if things got bad.

'Here we go,' said Reggie. 'Remember: stick close to me.'

'I'll remember.'

4

'Mister Dixon,' said Dupont. The fat bastard was all shining teeth and crocodile smiles tonight, Jeremy noted. 'We meet again.'

'Dupont,' Reggie replied, making no effort to pronounce the name correctly. If Dupont minded, he made a good show of hiding it.

'Let's get straight to business, shall we?' said the Frenchman. 'I take it you have the money?'

Reggie grunted. 'I have it. Do you have the goods this time?'

'You need to ask? Mister Dixon, I am shocked. I really am.'

'After the shit you pulled, you're damn right I'm asking. I

lost good men because of your fuckup.'

Dupont stepped forward and seemed to grow in size. 'I don't care for your insinuations, Mister Dixon.'

'Fuck you,' Reggie spat. While Jeremy had fought against his instinct to grab at his gun when Dupont moved, Reggie had not so much as flexed a pinkie. 'You want to make this trade or not? I don't have all night.'

'I'm afraid not, Mister Dixon. Not with you, at any rate.'

For the first time, Reggie's mask slipped and Jeremy saw the morass of rage that boiled beneath the surface. In a blink of an eye, it was gone.

Jeremy knelt and made as if he was fastening his shoelaces.

'What are you talking about?' asked Reggie. 'You want to deal in this town, you deal with me. There's no one else. Get up, Pellie. For fuck's sake try to look professional, will you?'

Jeremy stood. 'I'm sorry, Reggie.'

'So you bloody should be. For fuck's sake man, we're supposed to be...'

His voice trailed off when his eyes latched on to the gun in Jeremy's hand. He began to ask what Jeremy thought he was playing at, but he did not have the time.

Jeremy squeezed the trigger three times. Reggie's body shuddered as each bullet cut deep into his chest.

He sank to the floor, coughing up blood and curses.

Finish him. The voice echoed in his head. He recognised it but did not know from where.

Remember what he did to you. Finish him now!

He raised the gun to the old man's head, and fired.

5

'Shots fired! Shots fired!'

The panicked cry came through the radio as Gretl ran down a grey-walled corridor toward the fire escape. It was Carter's voice, she could tell despite the interference. The guy clearly could not hold his own in a tense situation. He would get someone killed one day, that was for sure.

Hopefully he would not do it tonight.

She burst through the fire escape, grabbed the railing and leapt over it. The gravel crunched beneath her feet as she landed, and again as she rolled forward; stopping in a crouch and leaping to her feet. Over the commotion now going on in the yard, she doubted anyone would notice. Nevertheless, from here on in she needed to be careful.

Allemand was here. Allemand would hear her coming.

She looked around, scanning the area for trouble; for places anyone might hide now the shit had most definitely hit the fan; for places where she could sneak through the shadows and reach her man. Baron would take care of Dupont and the others, she only needed to deal with Allemand. He was the wildcard the Ministry were ill equipped to handle. If she did not catch him before he made his move, no one would leave the yard alive.

Keeping low and sticking to the shadows, she made her way into the yard.

6

The night was not going as Seth Baron had planned. Then again, few nights did. He had expected problems, but when the emaciated dogsbody had shot the city's most powerful drug lord, he knew there was no way he was getting the upper hand without a fight.

Carter stuck close to his left flank as they approached the entrance to the yard. Seth kept his eyes on the gunman, ready to fire if things turned nasty again. At present, it was a stand-off, just lots of angry chatter. Nobody wanted to make the first move. That was fine by him.

Carter moved to the left side of the entrance. Seth took the right side. Crouched and with his gun drawn, he waited for his backup to move in.

7

'That was a brave thing you did there,' said Dupont. 'There are going to be many men after you tonight.'

Jeremy Pellier looked down at the corpse piled at his feet, then at the fat man in the expensive suit. He was right. People would be out for his blood, and not just tonight. From here on in, he had to watch his back.

'You're going to need help just to stay alive,' Dupont continued.

'That sounds like an offer,' said Jeremy.

The Frenchman snorted. Jeremy did not understand the response.

'What do you want?'

'Fifty percent. Of everything.'

'Pull the other one,' Jeremy sneered. 'No one in their right mind would take that. Try harder.'

'Mister Pellier, I am trying to be reasonable here. The cost of setting up a new boss in this town will be significant, even someone as reasonably well connected as you already are. If you want to work with us – and I assure you, you do want to work with us – then you have to accept our terms. Fifty percent, or you can take your chances out on the street.'

Jeremy looked down at the old man's body. It had been so simple. Would his end come so easily?

'Thirty five,' he said, mustering as much force as he could convey.

The Frenchman shook his head.

Jeremy felt his grip on the gun slipping. His palms were hot and sweating; his shirt clinging to his back. He needed to finish this and soon, before more problems arose.

'Fine,' he said.

The Frenchman smiled. 'Then let's do business.'

8

'We're in position now,' said Travis through Seth's earpiece.

Seth said nothing in reply, but looked over at Carter, who nodded to him. Seth held up three fingers: move in on three. Carter nodded again.

Three.

Two.

One.

'Armed Government Agent!' called Seth as he stormed into the yard. 'Hands in the air!'

Pellier turned quickly, his gun raised. Carter shot him in the shoulder before Seth could react. The gun fell to the floor with the heavy thud of metal on concrete. Pellier clutched at the wound and screamed obscenities, but Seth hardly noticed. His eyes were fixed on Dupont. No one else mattered now.

No one except Allemand, wherever he might be. He was the rogue agent in all this. If the vampire woman did not hold up her side of the bargain, Allemand could prove their undoing.

He put those thoughts out of his mind and walked toward Dupont, his gun raised; ready to fire at the slightest provocation. Carter and the others cold deal with the monkeys, he wanted organ grinder all to himself.

Come on, you bastard. Give me an excuse.

But the fat Frenchman just stood there in his expensive suit, sucking on a cigarette and holding his hands up on either side of his bulbous head. His grey eyes followed Seth's every move but other than that, he said and did nothing.

'Marc Dupont, I am arresting you on suspicion of conspiracy in the murder of Craig Baron,' the words cut deep in Seth's throat. He held the gun so tightly it shook in his hand. *Do something, you bastard! Give me a reason. GIVE ME A REASON!*

'You do not have to say anything,' he heard himself say.

'But it may harm your defence if you do not mention when questioned something you later rely on in court.'

The fat man sniffed, and lowered his hands. 'Is that it?' he asked. The tone made it sound like he was almost bored.

Seth grabbed the man's arm and forced him against a packing crate. He reached into his jacket for handcuffs when he felt a hand on his shoulder. Suddenly he was spun around and a black gloved fist smacked into his face. He lost his footing, and fell. The gun slipped from his grip.

'Carter!' he called as Dupont's guard came at him again.

A shot rang out. The guard's eyes glazed, and he crumpled. Behind the falling man, Carter walked forward, his gun pointed at Dupont's head.

'No!' cried Seth, scrambling to his feet and pushing Carter away. The younger man fought to keep his footing, but at least he was pointing his gun at the ground now. 'He's mine! I want him alive!'

He could feel tears welling in the corners of his eyes. He brushed them away. There would be time for grief later. Right now, he had a job to do.

He felt the gun on the back of his head, and went cold.

9

Gretl crept toward the shadows where Allemand had been stood. She half expected that he would still be there, watching impassively as Baron's men dealt with his own. As she stepped off the gravel path onto the scuffed and stained concrete yard, her heart sank. Allemand was nowhere to be seen.

Her fists clenched. She closed her eyes, took a deep breath and swallowed her urge to scream. She had been so close! He had been right there in front of her and now? Nowhere. She had lost him again.

He could not have gone far, however. For all his years and all his skill, he could still not fly or just disappear into thin air. He had to be close by. She could still find him, if she hurried.

Someone grabbed her from behind; an arm around her shoulders, a hand grabbing her hair. Before she could react, her head was slammed against a shipping container. She staggered, saw stars, but steadied herself and turned around before her assailant could act again.

She halted for a brief second when her eyes fell on who had attacked her.

'Hans Allemand,' she said, slipping into the man's native tongue. 'I've been looking for you.'

'Your German needs some work,' said Allemand.

His comment took her by surprise; a fact Allemand played to his advantage. He stuck fast and low, slamming his fist into her gut. She doubled over in pain, sinking to her knees; steadying herself with one hand on the floor, the other clutching her stomach.

'Bastard,' she spat as she fought back the pain. She was well fed that evening, the pain would pass quickly.

As she climbed back onto her feet, he struck again. This time she was ready for him. She grabbed his arm as he lashed out, ducked under it and pulled around to his back, then kicked his right leg out from under him. He fell, and she fell with him; landing her left knee on the middle of his back, his arm still firmly in her grip.

For all his skills as a manipulator, Allemand's street fighting skills were severely lacking.

'I've been looking for you for a long time,' said Gretl.

'I don't care,' said Allemand. He struggled, but she held on tightly to him. He could not get free now.

'In fact, I've been looking for you since January of 1963. Do you remember where you were then?'

'Get off me, bitch. I'm going to fuck you up!'

'That's hardly an incentive for me to let you go then, is it?' Gretl said, as calmly as she could. 'I'll tell you where you were in January 1963. You were in Harderwijk. One evening, you came to my door claiming you had been robbed and needed me to call the Police.'

'Is this going anywhere?' asked Allemand. Gretl ignored him.

'You looked hurt. You were covered in blood. I took pity on you, let you in. Do you remember what happened next?'

'No.' His voice was flat, almost bored.

Her heart sank. She knew it had been unlikely. He probably did all the things he did to her and her family to so many people. Why would she be different? Why would one more matter to him?

But it mattered to her. She felt a fire in her belly now. After decades of hunting, she had him and she was going to make him pay.

She leaned in close, still holding on to his arm. She would

be risking pulling it out of its socket now, but she simply did not care. She put her lips to his ear. She could feel him squirm as he tried to break free.

'Well *I* remember,' she said.

With her free hand, she pulled a syringe from her jacket pocket and in one swift stabbing motion, emptied its contents into Allemand's neck.

10

'Put the gun down,' said Dupont. 'Put it down slowly, and step away.'

'No,' said Carter.

'Do it or I'll blow his fucking head off.'

'And then he'll shoot you,' said Seth. 'Or if not him, one of the snipers.'

Dupont said nothing; and at that moment, Seth knew he would win. He lowered his hands and turned around slowly. Dupont was still holding the gun at his head and he did not feel confident enough to challenge him on that just yet, but that time was coming.

'It's over,' he said. 'Put the gun down and come quietly.'

Dupont shook his head. 'No.'

'There's really no good way out of this for you,' Seth continued. 'But it would be best if you came out of it alive.'

'Why? So you can have revenge for your son? Don't think I don't know why you're here. This was never about my deal, was it? It was about payback.'

'You're wrong,' said Seth. 'What you did to my family was

85

terrible, but I'm not here for that now. All I'm here for is to take you in.'

'No,' said Dupont. 'I'll not be some trophy, rotting in prison while you brag to your friends.'

'Look, we can do this– **No!**'

Seth lunged forward as Dupont turned the gun on himself. The shot echoed around the yard.

Seth's glasses smeared with blood and other things he did not care to identify. The dead man fell to the ground, and Seth dropped to his knees beside him.

'No!' he roared. 'Damn you, you bastard! Damn you!'

He pounded the corpse with all his might, pouring his grief and rage into every blow. His hands were red, his soul empty.

When Carter eventually pulled him to his feet, whatever had been left of Seth Baron had died.

11

Gretl dragged Allemand to his feet and hauled him into the yard. He staggered along beside her, his head lolling to one side and rocking as they walked.

Seth was sitting on the bonnet of Allemand's Mercedes. Carter stood beside him, smoking a cigarette and looking concerned. By the gates, two men in cheap grey suits were reading three men in expensive black suits their rights.

'You got your man, then,' said Carter, bitterly.

Gretl said nothing.

'What will you do now?' asked Seth. His voice sounded distant, like he had become detached from the world.

'We're going to wait for sunrise,' she said.

'Won't that kill you?' asked Carter.

Gretl looked at the young man, weighing up the likelihood that he meant what he had just said. She decided he did. He really was not the sharpest tack in the box.

'You never planned to come out of this, did you?' asked Seth.

'No. I want to see my family again,' she said.

Seth snorted a dry laugh but his face told her he found nothing about the situation all that funny.

'Go home,' she said. 'Go home to your wife. You can deal with this mess in the morning.'

Seth nodded slowly.

Carter put his arm around his boss' shoulders and led him away.

Chapter Ten

1

'Good morning, Mister Allemand,' said Gretl.

She spoke in her native Dutch, and wore the same clothing she had died in almost fifty years ago. Some things defy logic and can only be described as sentiment. Today seemed an appropriate time for such sentiments.

'What the fuck did you do to me?' asked Allemand, in German. His head was pounding, his limbs were numb and he could not move.

'A little tranquilliser,' said Gretl. She ignored his choice of language. The bastard could struggle through the effects of the drug to understand what she was saying. 'Well, a lot of tranquilliser, actually. Normally I would be careful about how much I use but I figured it wouldn't kill you so why bother?'

Allemand's mind cleared a little. He noticed he was sitting, tried to get up. His arms and legs were tied to a leather office chair.

'What are you doing?' he snarled. 'It's almost morning.'

Gretl shrugged. 'I know. Don't you miss it? It's been how long for you? A hundred years or so? For me it's not even been half that and I miss the daylight. I thought it would be nice to see it again, one more time.'

'I don't want to see the fucking daylight.'

Gretl put one hand on either of Allemand's shoulders and leaned in so close that their foreheads were practically touching.

'Then you shouldn't have killed my family.'

2

When they returned in the morning, all that remained was yellow police tape flapping in the wind, and a new charred mark on the concrete. The cleanup team had already been through to collect any remains. No doubt there were two silver-steel alloy urns being placed in deep storage right at that very moment.

'Think she actually did it?' asked Carter.

Seth stood with his hands buried deep in his coat pockets, staring blankly at the mark on the ground.

'Yeah,' he said. 'She'd spent too long chasing her man. When she got him, what else was there to live for?'

'You see, I just don't get that,' said Carter. 'There's always something to live for. It might not be obvious right there and then, but there's always something 'round the corner if you look hard enough.'

He pulled a packet of cigarettes from his pocket, lit one and offered the packet to Seth. The older man shook his head.

'Let's hope your right,' said Seth, although from his tone it was clear he did not mean it.

Carter patted the old man on the shoulder. 'Come on, let's go and get breakfast. It's my shout.'

Zoë Robinson

Want more from the world of dark fantasy?
Slake your thirst on this first chapter of
Curse of the Other World
The forthcoming novel by Zoë Robinson

Zoë Robinson

Curse of the Other World

1

Peter wiped the blood and vomit from his unconscious friend's mouth and knew that today was not going to be a good day. There were certain things he would do for a friend but cleaning them up after a night of abusing themselves was not on his list. Nevertheless, he cradled Kate's head in his arm and checked her pulse. It was slow and weak but steady. She would live long enough for him to lecture her about irresponsibility.

The bathroom floor was not the place for a woman as ill as Kate was to be sleeping so Peter scooped her up in his arms and carried her through to the bedroom. It was a short walk since despite all her family's wealth, she lived in a tiny flat over a Post Office that had been closed for two years. She might be a callous bitch with no regard for her physical wellbeing, or the wellbeing of anyone else for that matter, but if there was one thing she did well, it was stubbornly refuse to spend more money than she actually needed to.

The bedroom was small, perhaps twelve feet square, and dominated by a double bed with deep purple sheets. The wall opposite the window was taken up by a fitted wardrobe, the wall with the door in it was lined entirely with bookshelves. Peter ignored the books for the time being, knowing their contents were not to his tastes, and laid Kate on the bedsheets. Her eyes flickered behind closed lids, but she made no efforts to open them.

'Get some rest,' he told her.

'Where am I?' she asked. Her voice was dry and little more than a whisper.

'You're in bed. Get some rest.'

'I've got something I need to show you,' she said.

'Later,' he replied but he may as well have held his tongue. Kate's breathing was slow and regular and she lay perfectly still on the bed. She was asleep.

Peter pulled a blanket from the wardrobe and covered her with it, having decided this was the better option to waking her by pulling out the duvet she was laid on top of. Then he pulled a second blanket out for himself, closed the wardrobe and walked to the small lounge to settle down on the sofa for a few hours' rest. It was eight in the morning and Kate was a late riser even at the best of times, so he could probably get four or more hours of shut eye before she started moving again.

That was fine by him. He had been working long hours over the last three weeks, dealing with an over-full accident and emergency unit. That was not his usual area but when a sudden rise in morons fighting in bars, or the streets, or each other's homes, flared up like what had happened recently, it was all hands on deck.

No sooner had his head hit the cushions he had stacked up on one end of the sofa he was startled awake by a clashing sound in the kitchen. Someone was making tea by the sound of things. What time was it anyway? He checked his watch.

13:15. He had been asleep for around five hours. The person in the kitchen must be Kate.

He threw the blanket off himself, rubbed his eyes with his massive hands and staggered into the kitchen, still bleary from having woken so suddenly. Kate was by the kettle, pouring boiling water into a teapot and using her left index finger to check when the pot was nearly full. She put the kettle down quickly and sucked on her finger while she felt for the lid of the teapot.

'Tea?' she asked, without looking around.

'Sounds great,' said Peter.

'There's cereal in the cupboard if you want some.'

'Tea will be fine, thanks.'

Kate carried the teapot over to the kitchen table, navigating the short distance from counter top to table with care and carrying the pot with both hands. Peter knew from experience that asking her if she needed help would only serve to annoy, her pride in her own self sufficiency being one of her most prized possessions, so he simply took a seat at the table and waited for her to finish pouring out the tea.

'What was it you wanted to see me about?' he asked as he sipped the hot, black liquid. He always took his tea without milk, to preserve the flavour. Kate, on the other hand, doused her tea in so much milk he was surprised it was still warm when she finally drank it.

'A video,' said Kate. 'I need your opinion on whether it's fake.'

Peter raised an eyebrow. Kate stared vaguely at him, as if waiting for him to react.

'Why would it be fake?' he asked.

'Because despite my years of study, I have never seen a dead man make a video before.'

2

The video was grainy and contained more jump-cuts than Peter could possibly count, as if it was cut-and-pasted together from a larger video. Despite this, the figure on the screen looked, acted and sounded just like Daniel. It was shocking for Peter to see someone he had known well for many years, someone he had been with when he died, talking to him now.

'You'll have to excuse the poor quality,' said Kate. 'There's a lot of interference on here. I tried to clean it up but there's only so much you can do with this digital crap.'

'It looks like there's a second person here.' Peter paused the video and pointed to a point on the screen just to the left of Daniel. 'I think that's an arm.'

Kate peered at the screen, getting so close that her nose was in danger of being squashed against the display. 'I don't see anything.'

'It's definitely there. Someone wearing a suit jacket.'

'A suit? That's not something Daniel would have been seen dead in. Well, okay, he was seen dead in one at the funeral but that was hardly his choice.'

'Kate, don't talk like that.'

'Hmm? What's wrong? Oh. Right.'

Kate's fingers flew across the keyboard, tapping commands into the system.

'What are you doing?'

'Zooming in and slowing the film down.'

The video started to play again, moving slowly and showing up a very definite flickering on Daniel while the room he was standing in remained fixed on the screen. Occasionally, glimpses of a second person appeared for a brief second.

Peter tapped his fingers on the desk while he mulled over some ideas in his head. 'It's almost as if there's a second video here. Maybe suit guy recorded his video over the top of Daniel's and someone just cut out all the bits with Dan in to make this clip?'

'That's a nice theory,' said Kate. 'Provided you think this is a digitized copy of a video cassette.'

'You sound like you don't believe that.'

Kate shook her head. 'Look at how the video blocks when you zoom in on it. This is a 720 pixel, high definition video recording. There's no film grain and no evidence of hum, whine or audio distortion associated with recording VHS to a computer or DVD. This video was taken on a small digital camcorder or a mobile 'phone.'

'You can tell all that just by looking at a few frames close-up?' asked Peter.

'No,' said Kate. Her voice was more icy than normal. 'I spent last night analyzing the audio and video content to confirm my theory.'

'Then why am I here looking at it all again?'

'A second opinion is sometimes useful. You spotted Suit Man, didn't you? I hadn't seen him.'

She patted him on the shoulder and slumped onto a sofa covered in blankets to hide the worn out leather on the cushions and arms.

'Okay,' she said. 'Theories?'

'Aside from the obvious?'

Kate gave Peter a look that would make even the sternest of old-fashioned schoolteachers nervous. 'And what, exactly, is "the obvious", bearing in mind that I've already ruled out the possibility that this is a fake?'

Peter turned away from the computer and walked to one of the two armchairs beside a fire that had not been lit in all the time he had known Kate. One armchair was full of books, a piece of wood and a very dangerous-looking knife with an ornate bone handle. Peter sat in the other chair.

'Okay then,' he said. 'Amaze me with your intellect.'

Kate ignored the implied sarcasm. Still laid on the sofa, she launched into a tirade of facts, observations and deductions.

'The video is high definition but only 720p, which means it is filmed on either a camera phone or a cheaper video camera; which is borne out by the lower grade film quality. The sound quality is consistent throughout, so the person in the video is the person speaking rather than a dub overlayed during editing. There are numerous jump-cuts but the lighting in the video does not change, so it was recorded in one take. The room is decorated in the same manner as Daniel's bedroom in the house he rented when he died. Conclusion? The video is edited to remove the person who was supposed to be in the recording, because Daniel is video interference. Daniel wants to send me a message and someone agreed to help him.'

'Who?' Peter asked. Trying to argue with Kate about the possibility that Daniel was not sending messages from beyond the grave was useless, so he did not even try.

'Whoever was originally recording the video. The man in the suit.'

'And why would he want to help a dead man talk to you?'

Kate sighed. 'Because Daniel is warning us about Coxton Hall.'

'Oh for fuck's sake, Kate!' Peter shouted. 'Are we going to go through this bloody thing again? It's been *eight years!*'

'Shouting at me won't change the facts,' said Kate. Her tone of voice did not change, remaining as flat and disinterested as ever.

'Just let it go, will you?'

'The question is,' said Kate as she clambered unsteadily off the sofa and made her way back to the computer. 'Why now? You're right that it has been eight years, plus two months and seventeen days to be exact, since Daniel died. Why is he showing up now?'

She slumped into the chair in front of the computer desk, the twenty year old metal joints creaking under her weight. She was nine stone at most but the chair had never been oiled in all the time Peter had known her. If there was one thing she was exceptionally bad at, it was maintaining things in good condition.

Peter sighed and resigned himself to the fact that he was going to be dredging up bad memories for the next few weeks, until Kate either solved this mystery she had conjured up, or got distracted by the next pet project.

He leaned over at the desk beside her and watched as she trawled through the available information about the video and its mystery poster, *CalvinHobbes86*.

'Okay,' he said. 'Let's find out who this guy is.'

www.ingramcontent.com/pod-product-compliance
Lightning Source LLC
Chambersburg PA
CBHW072358190626
46811CB00019B/1368